The Fox and the Stork

Gerald McDermott

Green Light Readers
Harcourt, Inc.
Orlando   Austin   New York   San Diego   Toronto   London

Long ago, there was a fox who lived in the forest. Fox liked to play tricks on his friends.

One morning, Fox rowed his boat across
the pond. He saw his friend Stork. "Would
you like to come to my house for dinner?"
he asked.

"How kind of you to ask!" said Stork.
"Yes, I would like that."

That night, Stork rowed her boat across the
pond. She walked along the forest road. Then
she tapped on Fox's door with her long bill.

"Come in," said Fox. "I made soup!"
"I like soup," said Stork.

Fox and Stork sat down to eat. Fox didn't put the soup in a bowl. He served it on a flat dish.

Fox felt very smart. Stork couldn't eat
from the flat dish. All she could do was
dip the tip of her long bill into the
soup. Fox soon slurped it all up!

Stork was still hungry, but she didn't complain.

"Thank you for the dinner," said Stork. "Come to my house, and I'll make dinner for you."

The next day, Fox rowed his
boat to Stork's house.

"I don't like to boast," said Stork, "but my soup is the best. I use greens that grow in my own garden."
"Wonderful! Let's eat!" said Fox.

Stork put the soup in a tall jar. Fox didn't get a drop. All he could do was lick the top of the jar. Stork dipped in her long bill and drank it all up.

Fox moaned as he rowed home.
"I'm so hungry! This is my reward
for tricking a friend!"

At last Fox saw that being kind
to others is the right thing to do.

Think About It

1. How does Fox trick Stork?

2. How does Stork teach Fox a lesson?

3. What lesson does Fox learn?

4. Think about a friend who has been kind to you.

Be My Guest

Fox and Stork invited each other to dinner.

**Pretend that you are Fox or Stork
and make a dinner invitation for a friend!**

paper

crayons or markers

What: Dinner
Where: Fox's house
Time: 6:00 PM
Please Come!

1

Fold the paper
in half.

2

Write the
invitation.

3

Draw a picture on the front.

4

Give your invitation to a friend.

Have a pretend dinner and act out the Fox and Stork story.

A New Tale

Maybe Fox and Stork will be friends forever! Write about something they do together.

More About Storks

Storks are interesting birds. See what you can find out about them. Share what you learn with a friend.

Meet the Author-Illustrator

Gerald McDermott likes to retell myths and folktales because these stories have special messages for people of all ages. He uses his pictures to help tell the story and get the message to his readers.

Gerald McDermott hopes that you enjoy reading *The Fox and the Stork* as much as he did retelling it.

www.HarcourtBooks.com

First Green Light Readers edition 1999
Green Light Readers is a trademark of Harcourt, Inc., registered in the
United States of America and/or other jurisdictions.

The Library of Congress has cataloged an earlier edition as follows:
McDermott, Gerald.
The fox and the stork/Gerald McDermott.
p. cm.
"Green Light Readers."
Summary: A retelling of the La Fontaine fable in which
a stork finds a way to outwit the fox that tricked her.
[1. Fables. 2. Storks—Fiction. 3. Foxes—Fiction.]
I. La Fontaine, Jean de, 1621–1695.
II. Title. III. Series.
PZ8.2.M15Fo 1999
[E]—dc21   98-55238
ISBN 0-15-204877-4
ISBN 0-15-204837-5 (pb)

A C E G H F D B
A C E G H F D B (pb)

Ages 5–7
Grades: 1–2
Guided Reading Level: G–1
Reading Recovery Level: 16

Green Light Readers
For the reader who's ready to GO!

Five Tips to Help Your Child Become a Great Reader

1. Get involved. Reading aloud to and with your child is just as important as encouraging your child to read independently.

2. Be curious. Ask questions about what your child is reading.

3. Make reading fun. Allow your child to pick books on subjects that interest her or him.

4. Words are everywhere—not just in books. Practice reading signs, packages, and cereal boxes with your child.

5. Set a good example. Make sure your child sees YOU reading.

Why Green Light Readers Is the Best Series for Your New Reader

• Created exclusively for beginning readers by some of the biggest and brightest names in children's books

• Reinforces the reading skills your child is learning in school

• Encourages children to read—and finish—books by themselves

• Offers extra enrichment through fun, age-appropriate activities unique to each story

• Incorporates characteristics of the Reading Recovery program used by educators

• Developed with Harcourt School Publishers and credentialed educational consultants